Uncle Robbie's Magic

Mia has an Uncle Robbie, who does magic tricks. He can turn a red hanky into a green one, then into a purple one. Once, he made an egg appear from Mia's ear. Another time he used magic to pull a giant umbrella out of a hat. He can even make a sparkly silver ball float through the air.

Whenever Uncle Robbie comes to visit, he brings a new trick. One day it was a magic green wallet. He held out a pack of cards and said, "Pick one, Mia. Pick any card."

Mia pulled out the King of Hearts.

"Now," said Uncle Robbie, "tear it into bits."

Mia giggled. "Tear it up?" she asked.

"Yes, go on, rip it up!"

So Mia ripped it into tiny pieces.

"Now put the bits into my magic green wallet," Uncle Robbie told her. "And say the magic words, *wibble dibble.*"

"Wibble dibble," repeated Mia.

Uncle Robbie waved his magic wand over the wallet then opened it up. Inside was the King of Hearts, all stuck back together again.

"How did you do that?" gasped Mia.

"Ah, it's a tricky one," said her uncle. "You just have to believe in magic."

As well as magic, Uncle Robbie does lots of other fun things with Mia. He makes up treasure hunts, and hides gold chocolate coins around the garden.

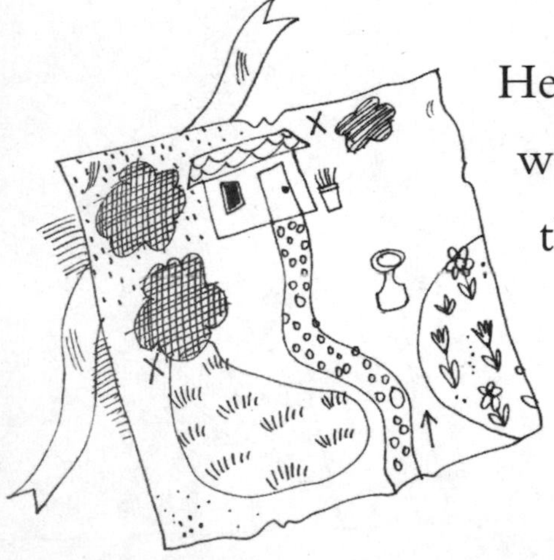

He always draws wonderful maps for the treasure hunts, rolled up and tied with ribbon.

Once, he made Mia a puppet theatre out of an old cardboard box. It had red curtains, and when you pulled a silver cord, they really opened and closed.

Uncle Robbie can't walk, so
he has a wheelchair to get around.
The wheelchair has coloured lights
that glow in the dark.

Mia likes sitting on his knee and having a ride. Sometimes she races him on her bicycle.

At Christmas Uncle Robbie decorates his wheelchair with tinsel, and Mia puts snowflake stickers all over it.

When Uncle Robbie is out with Mia, in the park or at the sweet shop, sometimes children come up to him and ask, "Why are you sitting down?"

Their mums go pink, but Uncle Robbie just smiles and replies, "It's because I have spaghetti legs. My legs are wibbly-wobbly, so I have these wheels instead."

One day a boy at the library asked him, "Can I *see* your spaghetti legs?"

Uncle Robbie laughed. "They look just like everybody else's legs," he explained. "But they're wobbly inside."

There are some days when Uncle Robbie gets very tired and needs a nap in the afternoon, just like Mia did when she was little. But when he wakes up, he smiles and says, "Ah, my magic powers are returning. How about a new trick?"

Mia's favourite is the Wobbly Wand trick. Uncle Robbie hands her a magic wand, but when she takes it from him, it turns all wobbly and bends in the middle.

"What have you done?" cries Uncle Robbie. "Give it back!"

Whenever he holds the wand, it straightens up again.

But every time Mia takes it, it flops right over!

One day Mia asked Uncle Robbie, "Why don't you magic your spaghetti legs into real walking legs?"

Her uncle smiled. "Ah, I haven't found the magic for that yet," he explained. "But I'm hoping that one day someone will discover how to do that trick."

Mia's Magic

Mia loves visiting Uncle Robbie and his cat, Treacle. Treacle is black with green eyes, and Uncle Robbie says she helps give him his magic powers. Mia loves stroking Treacle, and feeding her too.

One Friday after school, Mia and her mum took Uncle Robbie some cookies because he wasn't feeling well. Mia had baked them herself, so they were rather funny shapes and sizes, but her uncle didn't mind.

"Did you use magic ingredients?" he asked. "They're making me feel better already!"

While Mum did some gardening for Uncle Robbie, he and Mia sat munching the cookies.

But Mia was very quiet and looked worried.

"Is something wrong?" asked Uncle Robbie.

Mia sighed.

"My class is putting on a talent show at the end of term. We're all supposed to give a performance."

"But that sounds fun!" said Uncle Robbie.

"Not to me." Mia frowned. "I can't sing or dance, or anything like that, and I hate standing up in front of everybody."

"Oh, I'm sure there's *something* you can do," coaxed Uncle Robbie.

"There's *nothing*," replied Mia rather grumpily.

"Not even magic?" And Uncle Robbie gave her a big wink.

Mia's eyes grew wide.

"I could teach you a few tricks that will blow their socks off!" promised Uncle Robbie with a secretive grin. "How about it?"

"Could I wear a special sparkly costume?" asked Mia, cheering up a bit.

"Oh, I should think so," said Uncle Robbie. "The more glitter, the better!"

So the next day, Mum made Mia
a magician's cloak
out of an old shiny
purple dressing gown
sprayed with glitter
and Uncle Robbie
started to practise
tricks with Mia.

At first this did not go too well. Mia cut Grandpa's new tie in half, but couldn't magic it back together.

Next she tried the Rainbow Rope trick, but Treacle thought it was her new game and kept running off with the ropes.

Then there was a bit of a disaster with the Upside-Down Glass trick. Mia held a glass of coloured water, with a piece of card underneath, over Mum's head. When she pulled away the card, water poured all over Mum – who did not look too happy!

“I hope that won’t happen to your teacher,” she grumbled, going to fetch the hairdryer.

“Don’t worry, Mia,” laughed Uncle Robbie. “We just need a wee bit more practice.”

So they kept
trying every
evening, until at last
Mia was ready for
the big day.

"Your class will be amazed," Uncle Robbie told her. "But remember now, good magicians never reveal their secrets!"

On the day of the
talent show Mia
sat nervously
in class,
watching the
other children do
their performances.

Jamie played
a squeaky tune
on his violin.

Musab acted out
a scene from *Star Wars*,
with a lightsabre.

Millie
did ballet,
and Andrea
pretended
to be a
rock star.

When it was Mia's turn, she put on her sparkly cloak, and the teacher switched on the music she had brought. It was time!

First Mia
performed the
Rainbow Rope trick.
The class gasped when she waved her wand and turned three short coloured ropes into one long rainbow one.

They cried out in glee when she cut Jamie's school tie in half, then put it back together.

And they screamed as she held the Upside-Down Glass over their teacher's head. But this time, when she pulled the card away … no water fell out!

The class stared in amazement.

"How did you do that, Mia?" Jamie called out.

Mia smiled shyly. "My Uncle Robbie taught me," she said. "He knows all the best magic."

At playtime everyone crowded round Mia, begging her to teach them her tricks. But Mia just winked. "Sorry, good magicians never give away their secrets!"

Mia's Magic Card

Mia always has such fun with Uncle Robbie. But that summer she didn't see her uncle, or Treacle, for ages. His visits suddenly stopped, and they never went to his house any more. When Mia asked her mum why, she said that Uncle Robbie had not been very well.

"Is he better yet?" Mia asked Mum the next day, and every day after that.

One morning
Mum finally answered,
"Yes, he is much better now."

"Can we go and visit him? We can take magic cookies!" Mia begged.

"Well," Mum explained, "he doesn't want to see anyone just now, because he's feeling a bit sad."

"Why is he sad?" Mia wanted to know.

"Well ... sometimes he thinks he's not much use to anyone with his spaghetti legs," replied Mum. "Maybe you could make him a card to cheer him up."

Mia went to get her box of pens and coloured paper. She had an idea. She knew something *very* useful Uncle Robbie could do!

First she drew a card with a King of Hearts on the front. Then she added a magic wand and stuck glitter all around it.

"The glitter is the magic," she explained to Mum.

"He'll love that," smiled Mum. "I'll find an envelope for it."

When Mum wasn't looking, Mia wrote on the back of the card.

Please can you
come and do
your magic at my
birthday party.
You have the
very best magic!

Then she put the card in the envelope and stuck on a stamp. She and Mum posted it together.

A few days later, something arrived in the post for Mia. It was a letter, printed on gold notepaper, and it said:

Mr Spaghetti Legs

is pleased to announce that his

Spectacular Magic Show

will be coming to your party

at three o'clock

next Saturday.

Mia was so excited she did a cartwheel.

"Wow!" laughed Mum. "Isn't Uncle Robbie full of great ideas?"

Mia smiled secretly to herself. She knew whose idea it was really.

Later, Uncle Robbie phoned to ask if Mia and Mum could make a couple of things for the show. So Mum began to sew a gold tablecloth with stars on it, while Mia made a big sign from old cardboard. On it she painted the words **Mr Spaghetti Legs' Spectacular Magic Show** in purple letters, then stuck on lots of glitter.

On the day of the party
Uncle Robbie arrived with a large
bag of tricks and a twinkle in his eye.
"Happy birthday, Mia!"

He winked as he sat behind a table covered by the gold tablecloth. The glittery sign hung above his head, with balloons all around it.

"Hello, everybody!" grinned Uncle Robbie. "I have some very special magic for you today."

He did all his best tricks:
the Wobbly Wand,

the Ripped Card

and the
Floating
Sparkly Ball.

Mia was thrilled when she was asked to help with the Upside-Down Glass trick.

But there was also a new trick that Mia had never seen before.

“Now, as this is a birthday party,” said Uncle Robbie, “we’ll need a cake.” He took out a big silver pot and asked the children, “What do we need to make a cake?”

“Flour!” they shouted.

Uncle Robbie threw some daisies and buttercups into the pot.

“No, not *that* kind of flower!” they all cried.

"What else do we need?" Uncle Robbie wondered. "Eggs, you say?" He threw some eggs into the pot – only he forgot to take off the shells!

Finally he added raisins and jelly babies, then waved his magic wand.

Whoosh! Suddenly the pot was on fire, then all the ingredients turned into a delicious birthday cake for Mia – with icing and coloured candles!

Mr
Spaghetti

As the children clapped and cheered, Uncle Robbie whispered to Mia, “That was the most fun I’ve had in ages!”

“And it was the best birthday party ever!” laughed Mia.

Mia's friends loved Uncle Robbie's show so much that some of them asked him to come to their parties too. Mia's mum even made posters for **Mr Spaghetti Legs' Spectacular Magic Show**, and put them up in the supermarket and the library.

So now, whenever
Uncle Robbie is out and about,
children recognize him and say hello.

"Your uncle is amazing," Mia's friends tell her.

"Yes, he's magic," agrees Mia.